Within the fairy-tale treasury which has come into the world's possession, there is no doubt Hans Christian Andersen's stories are of outstanding character. Their symbolism is rich with character values. From his early childhood in the town of Odense, Denmark, until his death in Copenhagen, Hans Christian Andersen (1805-1875) wrote approximately 150 stories and tales. The thread in Andersen's stories is one of optimism which has given hope and inspiration to people all over the world. It is in this spirit that the Tales of Hans Christian Andersen are published.

THE FIR TREE
by Hans Christian Andersen
Translated from the original Danish text by Hans Henrik
Breitenstein
Illustrated by Tiziana Gironi
U.S. Edition 1988 by WORD Inc., Waco. TX 76702
Text: © Copyright 1988 Scandinavia Publishing House,
Nørregade 32, DK-1165, Copenhagen K. Denmark
Artwork: © Copyright 1988 Tiziana Gironi and
Scandinavia Publishing House
Printed in Portugal
ISBN 0-8499-8581-1

Hans Christian Andersen
The Fir Tree

Illustrated by Tiziana Gironi
Translated from the original Danish text
by Hans Henrik Breitenstein

WORD INC.
Waco, TX 76796

Out in the forest stood such a pretty fir tree. It had plenty of space and sunlight, there was fresh air, and round about grew many larger companions, both pine and fir. But the little fir tree had a burning desire to grow. It did not notice the warm sunlight or the fresh air, it didn't care about the peasant children, who went about chatting when they were out gathering strawberries or raspberries.

Often they passed by with full baskets or with the strawberries put on a straw. Then they would sit down by the little tree and say, "How small and pretty that one is." The tree did not like to hear that.

One year later it was a long shoot taller, and the year after that yet another much longer shoot had grown out. This is how you can tell how old a fir tree is, by the number of rings it has grown.

"Oh, if I only were a big tree, like the others!" the little tree sighed. "Then I could spread out my branches far and wide, and with my top look out into the wide world. Then the birds would build their nests amongst my branches, and when the wind blew I could nod as solemnly as the others over there."

It took no pleasure in the sunshine, the birds or the red clouds which sailed overhead every morning and evening.

Now it was winter and the snow lay sparkling white. Often a hare came bouncing along and jumped right over the little tree. Oh how annoying that was! But two winters passed, and by the third winter the tree was so tall that the

hare had to run around it. "Oh! To grow, to grow tall and old, that must surely be the only truly beautiful thing to do in life," the tree thought.

In the autumn the woodcutters always came and felled some of the tallest trees. It happened every year and the young fir tree, which was now wellgrown, trembled because the great majestic trees fell to the ground with loud cracks and crashes. The branches were cut off so they looked all naked, long and narrow. They were hardly recognizable. Then they were put on carts, and were pulled out of the forest by horses. Where were they going? What would happen to them?

In the spring, when the swallow and the stork came, the tree inquired of them, "Do you know where they were taken? Have you met them?"

The swallows knew nothing at all, but the stork nodded gravely and said, "Yes, I believe I have. I saw many new ships when I flew from Egypt. On the ships were grand masts, I dare say it must have been them, they smelt of pine. They send their greetings to you. Oh, how tall and straight they stand!"

"Oh, if only I were tall enough to fly across the sea! What is it like, this sea, what does it look like?"

"Well, that would take too long to explain," said the stork, and then he left.

"Enjoy your youth," the sunbeams said. "Enjoy your freshness of growth and the young life that is within you."

And the wind kissed the tree, and the dew cried its tears over it, but the tree did not appreciate it.

At Christmas time, the very young trees were cut down, trees which often were neither as tall nor as old as this fir tree that had no peace nor rest, but always longed to get away.

These young trees, who were the very prettiest and always kept their branches, were loaded on carts and drawn out of the wood by horses.

"Where are they going?" asked the young fir tree. "They are not taller than I. One of them was even much smaller. Why did they keep all their branches? Where are they being taken?"

"We know! We know!" the sparrows chirped. "We have looked through the windows down in the town. We know where they go. They are given the greatest pomp and glory one can imagine. We have looked through the windows and have seen how they are placed in the middle of a large, warm room, decorated with the loveliest things, like gilded apples, gingerbread, toys, and hundreds of candles."

"And then. . . ?" asked the tree, and a shiver went through all its branches. "So? Then what happens?"

"Well, that is all we saw. It was marvelous."

"I wonder if I was born to go this path of splendor?" the tree cried for joy. "That is even better than traveling across the sea. How my heart painfully yearns for it. How I wish it were Christmas. Now I am tall and spread out like the others that were taken away last year. Oh, if only I were on the cart. If only I were in the nice warm room with all its glory and splendor. And what would happen? Well something even better comes, even more wonderful. Why else would they adorn me such? There must be something even grander and more glorious! But what? Oh I ache, I long! I do not understand why I feel this way."

"Rejoice in me," said the fresh air and the sunlight, "rejoice in your youthful freshness out here in the open."

But the tree felt no joy. It grew and grew. Winter and summer it stood green, dark green it stood. People who saw it exclaimed, "It is a charming tree," and at Christmas it was the first tree to be felled.

The axe chopped deeply to the marrow, the tree fell to the ground with a sigh. It felt a pain, a helplessness, it was unable to think of any joy. It was sad to part with its old home, from the spot where it had sprouted. It knew it would never again see its dear old companions, the little bushes and flowers round about and maybe not even the birds. The parting was not at all pleasant.

The tree did not recover until it was unloaded in the yard with the other trees and heard a man say, "This is a fine tree, this is the only one we want."

Now two servants, all dressed in finery, came and carried the fir tree into a big, wonderful hall.

On the walls hung portraits and by the big open fireplace stood large Chinese vases with lions on their lids. There were rocking chairs, silk settees, large tables covered with picture books and toys worth hundreds and hundreds of dollars, at least that was what the children said. The tree was set up in a big sandbox. But nobody could tell that it was a sandbox because it was covered with a piece of green cloth, and it was placed in the middle of a large, colorful carpet.

Oh, how the tree trembled. What was going to happen? Servants and young ladies went about decorating it. On the branches they hung little bags cut from colored paper. Each bag was filled with sweeties. Gilded apples and walnuts hung as though they had grown there, and more than a hundred red, blue and white candles were fastened on the branches. There were dolls, looking like real people. The tree had never seen the likes of them before, covered in green, and at the very top was placed a big star made from gilded paper. It was splendid, absolutely splendid.

"Tonight," they all said, "tonight it will shine."

"Oh," the tree thought, "I wish it were evening, if only the candles were lit. What will happen then? Will there be trees from the forest coming to look at me? I wonder if the sparrows will fly past the windows? Am I going to grow roots here and stand decorated both winter and summer?"

Oh yes, it was sure of this. Yet it suffered a severe bark-ache from sheer longing, and bark-ache is as unpleasant for a tree as a headache is for the rest of us.

Now the candles were lit. What brightness, what glory. It made the tree shudder through all its branches, so that one of the candles set the green on fire! It scorched badly.

"God save us!" one of the ladies shouted and quickly put out the fire.

Now the tree dared not even quiver. How awful. It was so afraid of dropping any of its fineries. It was all giddy in this splendor. Then both the doors flew open and many children rushed in as if they were about to push over the tree. The older people followed calmly. The little ones stood silent, but only for a moment, then they started cheering again so their shouts rang out in the room.

They danced around the tree, and one after another, the gifts were plucked from the tree.

"I wonder what they are doing?" the tree thought. "What is going to happen next?" And the candles burned down to the branches. As they burned down they were quenched and then the children were allowed to plunder the tree. Oh, they jumped on it so that all the branches creaked and groaned. If the top and the gold star had not been tied to the ceiling, it would have tipped over.

The children danced with their wonderful toys. Nobody looked at the tree except the old nanny, who walked around peeking amongst the branches. But that was only to see if someone had left a fig or an apple.

"A story! Tell us a story!" The children shouted and pulled a short heavy man towards the tree, and he sat down beneath it. "For then we are out in the green wood," he said, "and it would do the tree good if it also listened. But I will tell only one story. Do you want to hear the one about Jack the Giant-Killer or the one about Simple Simon, who fell down the stairs, and yet was raised to honor and married the princess?"

"Jack the Giant-Killer!" shouted some. "Simple Simon!" shouted others. There was such a noise and commotion, only the fir tree was quiet. He thought, "Don't I get to join in, don't I get to do anything?" After all, it had been there and had done what it was supposed to do.

Then the man told the story about Simple Simon, who fell down the stairs and yet was raised to honor and married the princess. The children clapped and shouted, "Go on, tell us one more!" They also wanted to hear about Jack the Giant-Killer, but they only got the story about Simple Simon.

The fir tree stood quite still and deep in thought. The birds in the wood had never told stories like this. Simple Simon fell down the stairs and still got the princess. "Well, that is the way it goes in the world," the tree thought, and believed it was true because the man who had told the story seemed so nice.

"Well, who knows, maybe I will also fall down the stairs and marry a princess!" And it looked forward to the next day, to be dressed up with candles and toys, gold and fruits.

"Tomorrow I will not tremble," it thought. "I will enjoy all my magnificence. Tomorrow I will hear the story about Simple Simon again, and maybe the one about Jack the Giant-Killer. And the tree stood quietly, immersed in deep thoughts all that night.

In the morning the butler and the maid came in.

"Now the fun starts again," the tree thought. But they carried it out of the room, up the stairs and into the attic. And there, in a dark corner, with no daylight shining in, they left it.

"I wonder what this is supposed to mean?" the tree thought. "What am I supposed to do here? What will I get to hear?" Leaning against the wall it thought and thought. And there was plenty of time to think because nights and days passed. No one entered, and when finally somebody did come in, it was only to put some boxes away in the corner. The tree was quite hidden. It looked as if it were completely forgotten.

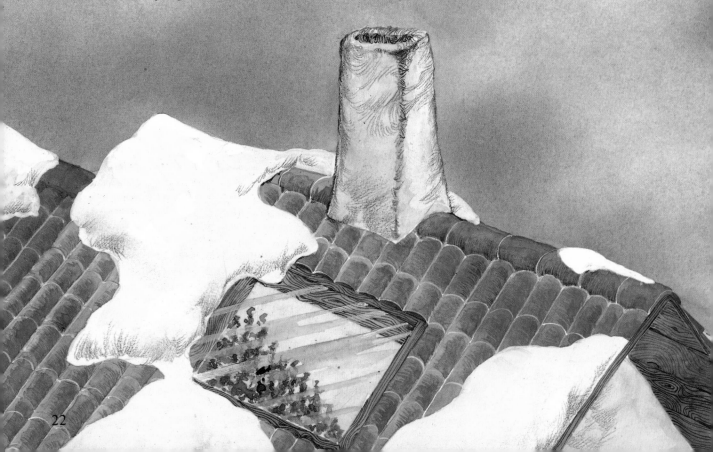

"Now it is winter out there," the tree thought, "the earth is hard and covered with snow, the people could not plant me. That is why I am kept here warm and comfortable until springtime. How considerate. How good the people are! If only it were not so dark and terribly lonely.

"What a terrible cold," the little mice said. "Otherwise this is a good place to be. Isn't that so, you old fir tree?"

"I am not at all old!" the fir tree said, "there are many much older than I."

There's not even a little hare. It was so nice out there in the wood, when the snow covered the ground and the hare bounced past. Even when he jumped over me it was nice, although I did not like it at the time. Up here it is so frightfully lonely!"

"Squeak, squeak," said a little mouse at that moment. He came out. Then another little mouse appeared. They sniffed at the fir tree and ran in among its branches.

"Where do you come from?" the mice asked, "and what do you know?" They were ever so curious. "Tell us about the loveliest place in the world. Have you been there? Have you been in the pantry, where cheeses are lined up on shelves, and hams hang from the ceiling, where you dance on tallow candles, enter skinny and leave bursting fat!"

"I don't know anything about that," the tree replied, "but I know the wood, where the sun shines and the birds sing." And then it told its story, everything from its youth, and the little mice had never before heard anything like it so they listened and said, "You have seen so much! How happy you must have been!"

"I?" the fir tree said, and reflected on what it had been telling about itself. "Yes, as a matter of fact those were rather jolly good days." But then it told them about Christmas Eve, when it had been decorated with gingerbread and candles.

"Oh!" exclaimed the little mice, "how happy you have been, you old fir tree."

"I am not at all old!" the tree protested. "It was only this winter that I came in from the wood. I am in the prime of my years, I have only just stopped growing."

"You are such a good storyteller," the little mice said, and the night after that they returned with four other little mice who wanted to hear the tree tell its story. The more it thought, the more it remembered, "What jolly days! But they may yet return, indeed they may. Did not

Simple Simon fall down the stairs, and even then marry a princess? Perhaps I, too, can have a princess." And then the fir tree remembered a pretty little birch tree that grew out in the wood. For the fir tree, this was a wonderfully lovely princess.

"Who is Simple Simon?" the little mice asked. And then the fir tree repeated the whole story. It remembered every single word and the little mice were so delighted they were ready to jump to the top of the tree.

The next night many more mice came, and on Sunday there were two rats. But they said that the story was dull, which made the little mice sad, for now they also liked it less.

"Do you only know that one story?" the rats asked.

"Yes, only that one," the tree replied. "I heard it on the happiest night of my life, but then I was not aware of how happy I was."

"It is an exceedingly uninteresting story! Don't you know any stories with bacon and tallow candles? No tales from the larder?"

"No," said the tree.

"Well, thank you very much" said the rats as they left.

Eventually the little mice also stayed away, and then the tree sighed. "It was so nice when they gathered around me, those nimble little mice, and listened to my story. Now that is over too! But I will remember to be happy when I am taken out again."

But when did this happen? Well, it happened early one morning, when some people came in and started rummaging through the attic. The boxes were moved, and the tree was pulled out. They did throw it a bit hard onto the floor, but straight away a servant carried it towards the stairs, where daylight shone.

"Now life begins all over again!" the tree thought. It felt the fresh air, the first beam of sunlight. Then it was out in the courtyard. Everything went so quickly, the tree forgot to look at itself, there was so much else to look at. The courtyard was next to a garden, and everything in it was in full bloom. The roses climbed fresh and fragrant over the little fence. The lime-trees blossomed, and the swallows flew about saying, "po-teeh-weet, my husband has arrived!" but they were not thinking of the fir tree.

"Now I shall live!" It said rejoicing and spread out its branches. Alas, they were all withered and yellow. It lay in the corner amongst the weeds and nettles. The golden paper star was still on its top and sparkled in the bright sunlight.

In the courtyard a couple of the merry children who had danced around at Christmas were playing. The smaller one ran over and tore off the golden star.

"Look what was still on that nasty old Christmas tree." He stepped on its branches so that they cracked beneath his boots.

And the tree looked at all the flowery splendor and freshness of the garden, and then it looked at itself and wished to be back in its dark corner in the attic. It remembered its fresh youth in the wood, the jolly Christmas Eve, and the little mice, who had been so happy to hear the story of Simple Simon.

"It is over, all over!" the poor tree said. "If only I had enjoyed myself when I could have. All is gone, all is finished."

Then the farmhand came and chopped the tree up into little pieces until there was nothing left but a small pile. It flared up nicely under the big brewing kettle, and it sighed so deeply, every sigh was like a faint shot.

This caused the children who were playing outside to run in and sit in front of the fire. They looked into it and shouted "Bang bang!" But with every crack which was a deep sigh, the tree thought of a summer's day in the wood, a winter's night when the stars were shining. It thought of Christmas Eve and Simple Simon, the only fairy tale it ever heard, and knew how to tell.

And then the tree was burned up and gone.

The boys played in the courtyard, and the smallest wore on his chest the golden star which the tree had worn on the happiest night of its life. Now the tree was gone, and it was all over, and so is this story. It had ended, yes ended. All stories do.

🔑 Study Key

The Fir Tree

Explaining the story:

The story of the little fir tree is a story of any human life. Often we do not appreciate what we are and what we have. We long for more, and by trying so hard to make our dreams come true we sometimes miss out on the happiness we already have. The tree was always dissatisfied and yearning for something more until it realized what it had lost. Then it began to long for the past.

Ask your parents or grandparents, and they will say, "Oh, my childhood and youth were the best times of my life. I wish I'd realized it then!" Learn from their experience and live as fully as you can now. Be happy about who you are and what you have. Someday you will realize how rich you really were.

Talking about the truth of the story:

What happens when we start to compare ourselves to others?

Find some places in the story that show what the fir tree longed for.

What do the Christmas decorations symbolize?

Show why the fir tree was unrealistic about itself and its future.

Applying the truth of the story:

Is it wrong to be optimistic and to try to realize one's dreams? In doing so, what should our attitude be?

What are your dreams?